Dear Parents:

Congratulations! Your child is taking the first steps on an exciting journey. The destination? Independent reading!

STEP INTO READING® will help your child get there. The program offers five steps to reading success. Each step includes fun stories and colorful art or photographs. In addition to original fiction and books with favorite characters, there are Step into Reading Non-Fiction Readers, Phonics Readers and Boxed Sets, Sticker Readers, and Comic Readers—a complete literacy program with something to interest every child.

Learning to Read, Step by Step!

Ready to Read   Preschool–Kindergarten
• **big type and easy words** • **rhyme and rhythm** • **picture clues**
For children who know the alphabet and are eager to begin reading.

Reading with Help   Preschool–Grade 1
• **basic vocabulary** • **short sentences** • **simple stories**
For children who recognize familiar words and sound out new words with help.

Reading on Your Own   Grades 1–3
• **engaging characters** • **easy-to-follow plots** • **popular topics**
For children who are ready to read on their own.

Reading Paragraphs   Grades 2–3
• **challenging vocabulary** • **short paragraphs** • **exciting stories**
For newly independent readers who read simple sentences with confidence.

Ready for Chapters   Grades 2–4
• **chapters** • **longer paragraphs** • **full-color art**
For children who want to take the plunge into chapter books but still like colorful pictures.

STEP INTO READING® is designed to give every child a successful reading experience. The grade levels are only guides; children will progress through the steps at their own speed, developing confidence in their reading.

Remember, a lifetime love of reading starts with a single step!

Step into Reading, Random House, and the Random House colophon are registered trademarks of Penguin Random House LLC.

Visit us on the Web!
StepIntoReading.com
randomhousekids.com

Educators and librarians, for a variety of teaching tools, visit us at
RHTeachersLibrarians.com

ISBN 978-0-399-55884-9 (trade) — ISBN 978-0-399-55885-6 (lib. bdg.)

Printed in the United States of America

10 9 8 7 6 5 4 3 2 1

STEP INTO READING®

2
STEP
READING WITH HELP

nickelodeon

RUBBLE'S BIG WISH

by Kristen L. Depken

illustrated by Harry Moore

Random House 🏠 New York

Rubble and Rocky
find an old box.
Rubble wants
to clean it up.
He takes a nap first.

Rubble has a dream.
He turns the handle
on the box.
A genie named Jeremy
pops out!
The box is magic!

The genie will give
Rubble three wishes.

Rubble wishes

for a bone

that will last forever.

The genie uses his magic.
A giant bone appears
in the sky!

Oh, no!
The bone crashes
through the roof
of the barn.

Rubble will
fix the roof.
The PAW Patrol
will help!

Rubble lifts the bone
with his crane.

Skye flies Rocky

to the roof.

Rocky fixes the roof.

Jeremy the genie helps.

The roof is fixed!
The pups chew
on the giant bone.

Oops!
Rubble falls
into a mud puddle.
He is so dirty!

Jeremy says Rubble

has two wishes left.

Rubble wishes

for a super bubble bath!

Rubble loves
his bubble bath.
It is so bubbly,
it floats away!

Oh, no!
Rubble's tub
gets stuck
in a tree.

The PAW Patrol will help!

Skye lowers Ryder.

He grabs Rubble

just in time.

Rubble has
one wish left.
He uses it
to thank his friends.

Jeremy flies
into the sky.
He gives the pups
tons of treats!